WIDE TIME

William Crane

www.widetimebook.com

First Edition
ISBN 978-0-9848482-2-5
Printed in the United States of America

To my true love, Rebecca

Author's Note: It may be the hiss of feedback coming through the speakers or a snare breaking through the mix, but music has always gone hand in hand with my writing. Whether it is to set the mood or finish off the day, it swirls like cream into coffee.

This collection has 13 tales. Each is paired with a song to enhance your experience and open a new window for your mind.

Read the words.

Find the songs.

Dig in deep.

William Crane
November 2014

WIDE TIME

The Belly of the Answer Man

I turn the shower on and the water warms my head. I close my eyes, but can see the drops touching my skin.

Tilting my head back, I feel the water rush over my skin and the wind drift in from the small window. I'm standing naked, but my mind dreams me up a scuffed pair of cowboy boots, a bolo tie and a plaid shirt to tie it together.

Where are my pants? I am dressed in dreams from the waist up. The dreams seem to follow my life. Voices are in languages strange and low. The words muffled in my mind like paper stacked in clumsy piles on my desk. Mountain vistas with rounded points instead of peaks. The summits offer no views, just clouds that are dark and dense.

I feel the stress well up in my stomach as I pull my head out from under the water. How have I gotten myself to this point? My work has me spinning like a dervish on a chain. My friends seem like rounded edges to me and I feel a little weaker every day.

That's why I love stepping in the shower and floating down.

"I'll be there soon enough," I tell myself.

I open my eyes and the black room surprises me. I forgot to turn on the lights again and stand there in the dark.

The water comes out of the showerhead in blues, greens, and reds. All the running colors tumble down and then at once, each stream finds its own way into my skin.

In what seems like both a moment and an eternity, I try each color. Red tones. Blue tones. Green tones. Black tones. Beige tones. A yellow tone. I hold my hand out and see streams of color-matched blood coursing through my veins. The color offers the only brightness in the bathroom during this early morning. The light shines in both brief moments and eternities.

My dream about being a pantless cowboy showering in the dark. It's time to wash the dust off. My bones fade away and the bolo melts back into my mind. The cowboy boots wash off my legs and down the drain in a liquid leather stream, spinning clockwise towards the center of the Earth.

I go with it.

This dream is its own and does not take its cue from my jagged mind. I let go and drift. I'm good at that. A plant hangs in the bathroom in the upper left corner. It must spend its days staring at the showerhead. For a second, I can see it waving its wisps. Goodbye.

"Yes, I'll be there soon enough," I repeat.

The color streams melt me down like metal for a smith. I float down the drain and into a darker darkness.

The water spins one way, over and over and down. The darker darkness spins together in all directions as its silence quiets the hum of my dreaming mind.

As I drift down with the color streams, I feel him next to me. He's always here at this point. Maybe he's just drifting too? It's too dark to tell, but the energy pulses steady. I imagine his eyes would glow in deep colors—an outlaw in black with spurs, a saddle and a silver pistol.

He reaches out his hands and places them over my eyes and closes my mouth before I can give him an answer to a question he has not asked yet. It is always the case on mornings like this, so I dive deeper down underneath the stream.

His hands lift off my mouth and he turns around. This is as deep as he wants to go, but I'm not done yet.

"Yes, I'll be there soon enough," I tell him as I imagine him floating up, half-formed, back up into the colors.

Sometimes opening my eyes can be hard, but it's easier to open them when it's dark in the room. Without the reflecting multi-colored water, it would be hard to know whether my eyes are even open.

The dark is always a strange place to be. My dad used to take us to caves when I was little. Big caves. Small caves. Popular ones. Ones that no one had discovered yet. Every weekend a different journey inside the earth. The strange thing is that it seems like nothing ever changes in a cave, but really it is just a rock pocket ready to collapse.

Sometimes I sleep for days, in fits of perpetuity. Sometimes, my work keeps me up, for the whole night. This morning, I've been up for what feels like 17 years, but it could be just two or three minutes. My hand shakes and it reaches out, half-formed, from the water driving down in the darkness.

I keep my eyes shut tight and dive into darker and deeper recesses. The water flows in spirals now. I reach out my hand, but can feel nothing on the edges.

I feel the downward motion bottom out in a pool. My feet cannot touch and I know that if I let it go, I would sink. But that would take effort. I float in the darkness and hear the water splash next to me.

The next stranger takes my hand. It's too dark to see her, but the water radiates with heat. She mainlines a language that I've never spoken, but I know all the words. The words leave her mouth in electrical waves. They pass through my eyes and ears as we talk about time and colors and cowboys. Cowboys wouldn't make good sailors, but some must have known how to swim. The electric words glow in the darkness and I see that the pool is slanted and we start to slide down. As we talk about how colors look without light, I notice it is even darker now, the words no longer glow and the water lost its color with the first man who floated up and away.

She smiles as if she's been with me the whole time in the water. Down through the darkness and floating in the bottomless pool. Her waves and my waves are electric words. If my ears worked at this depth, I'm sure there would be a buzzing between us. I always like running into her, except when she asks a question. I have no answers in the dark.

"You'll be there soon," she says.

"Yes, I'll be there soon, enough," I tell her.

The bright lights of the electric words shake my brain. They smell like the burning borders of my mind. They scream their own way, but I know she is my love in that instant, but her up is my down and I'm going down further than she is. My body feels stuck floating in the slanted pool, but she floats upward. I can never hold on to her for long, but this is the way it is supposed to be.

For a few seconds, I feel the warm water tap on the surface. I squeeze my eyes harder as I travel down deeper. I peel back the hued colors of my brain.

I try to remember how often I go down here, but can't seem to find the answer.

Maybe I've always been here, driving deeper and deeper. I try to close my eyes, but in the dark, how can you tell?

"Yes, I'll be there soon enough," I repeat to myself.

My life feels rotten sometimes, but never down here. My mind aches thinking about numbers and speaking words. If people were electric, it would be easier for me. The darkness hides me as I float down in the bottomless pool. I remember this part.

I remember this all and now I am almost there. This is an eternity and an instant for me. The colors return and bleed together. As I sink deeper under the water, I see colors drifting just above the surface. My hands grasp for them.

I reach for the colors, but can't reach them. I never can, but I always like to try. When I reach the bottom, maybe I can finally look over the edge.

No other strangers are down here. The colors never drift in the water.

I reach down into the darkness and push myself into the darker deep.

"Yes, I'll be there, soon enough," I think.

"Black Sheep"
SRC (1968)

A dark trip with mystic voices that float over the organ. The whispered background vocals give way to a guitar that burns through the speakers. The guitar pierces the song patiently while holding it together. The song tells a tale of living upside down where you are not really what everyone else is.

With each listen, the song hooks in a little deeper. The words spark mystical thoughts, the guitar focuses them and the drum floats you along to find what you were never looking for in the first place.

Animals in Our Own Time

Gods they were, but not really. Depends on how one looks at it. But isn't everything a matter of perspective? One of those eternal questions that only gods know the answer to. Well, at least the good gods.

Ash and Love were not good gods. They were stranded at a pit stop in some lonely galaxy. Love scribbled words in the dust with a stick. She always kept her words to herself and Ash.

"Something was always fucked. Somewhere," she said.

Ain't that the truth, Ash thought.

Ash grabbed the stick to stake his claim to eternal scribbles in dust. He stood there, chicken-scratching at the ground with the stick.

"The universe was dry." Ash wrote.

Love shook her head. Ash was never the most eloquent god, but he knew how to get things done, like skipping town. She was the talker and could weave her way out of any situation.

Their whole escape plan was Ash's idea in the first place. Love brought the drinks and the conversation. Her contributions to this interstellar getaway were necessary, if a little shallow.

Ash and Love were not good gods. Not even average gods. They didn't spin out fear and faith in equal measure while keeping their subjects in line. Nope. They lived with a capital L. Raced through space. Talked and drank. Drank and talked. Everywhere they made a mess in the space dust. Eternity wasn't a box big enough to hold Ash and Love.

With every peak, Ash and Love seemed destined for an equally deep valley. When Love dreamed, she would strain her eyes and see Ash at the bottom of a valley. He always was there for Love, especially when the drinks were too much and she could hardly stand. Love was there for him too, when he needed a little hope or a turn of phrase to impress their friends.

Standing at the phone booth, he stared into the receiver. No one on the other end of the line to accept his call. Ash and Love were stranded.

"C'mon, baby." He pleaded with Love for a little patience.

He asked the usual questions.

"What are we doing?"

"What were we doing?"

"What are we going to do?"

Here they were again.

They both laughed with regret. Did it really matter? Energy consisted of what they wanted it to be anyways. But the questioning went on and on. If only they were both circular thinkers, this whole interstellar debate could be avoided. Ash and Love were bummed out over the whole past, present and future. They had fucked up their last genesis. Ash, through his laziness. Love just didn't give a shit.

"Really, though, who hasn't fucked up?" Love coughed. Her breath turned to ice in this lonely galaxy.

"Not us," replied Ash.

That was true.

"Something was always fucked, somewhere." Ash and Love knew it to be one of those granite factoids.

Right now, this somewhere was two gods debating the finer points of planet building, conversing and hurtling through the void. Love was drunk and Ash was in denial.

Their last planet was nothing special, but to these two Gods it was something. Planets were not just playthings, not like when Ash and Love were young. It took time, care and heart to mold a globe.

Love didn't care for that much. Time spun around and around, but not quite at the point where she caught it. She spun too fast for her thoughts, with each thought seeming just out of reach. Her work always felt lopsided, with too much and too little to survive on her hemispheres. Balance was a hallmark of any good god.

Ash loved to stare while she spit at the perfect circle. His hemispheres reflected a balance between laziness and indifference, assuming that the inhabitants would just figure it out for themselves.

Their last planet melted down much quicker than they had envisioned. The souls screamed and kicked and died on a recycled course to another atom. So much death and disease, hatred and hell. It was too much for Ash and Love to take.

Haunting dreams were a beautiful masterpiece compared to the planet Ash and Love were running away from. The one they sent to a quick destruction.

Ash and Love thought about those poor souls. Those silly creatures put too much stock in their creators. Those fools created elaborate stories rooted somewhere between pure fiction and plain bullshit. Their safe harbor in a deep sea of hell. The need to believe that the blood red seas were not really boiling and that their bones wouldn't turn back to dust.

Ash and Love weren't happy about the ways things turned out. But they also weren't going to be the ones who would break the news to those poor fuckers that the whole thing was doomed from the very beginning.

"Something was always fucked, somewhere."

Ash and Love were fed up. They were no good at this. They realized it at the same time: It was time to say goodbye to their last lost planet and to each other.

"Eternity's a long time to spend with someone you can't stand," Love said to Ash.

"And with someone who is a complete fucking drunk," Ash shot back.

If one thing was true about gods and men and women, it's that none of us have much time to waste. They knew this a little more than most, but not by much. Ash and Love spun on the same coil. Their coil spun past their peer's creations at light-splitting speed.

Destination unknown.

Love was full of questions. Ash never took the time to answer them.

"Are we not Gods?"

"Are we not men?"

"Or women?"

"Are we not animals?"

"Well, we are."

"We are animals in our time."

Ash found a truth in this dimension where they were stranded. Ash and Love were animals. Ash may not have been the fastest beast, but he was methodical and could always find the next meal. Love was fierce, fast and vicious, but could quickly turn the land into desert.

They were gods of gods in their own time. Lesser gods wondered how they could both make a planet whole with only their teeth. The planet's inhabitants were smarter than spring flowers and the atmosphere was fresh and clean like a Monday morning mind. That time was long past, but Love and Ash would give anything for a taste of it right about now.

Somewhere, they had lost the plot.

"A diluted pool of eternal wisdom," Love shouted.

"You're drunk," Ash shouted back.

"So?" she thought to herself.

After all, Ash was drunk too, Love thought. Why was it all on her?

No one told Ash and Love how to be Gods. All those tiny fuckers flung their lives onto their shoulders. Ash and Love created the place. The warm, circular ball of shit. The creatures nuzzled right in. This was a planet for them to nestle in. What else could they do?

It was all too much. No wonder Love loved to drink. It kept the thoughts from flooding in. Ash couldn't stop the flood, no matter how much he drank. Wave after wave after wave after wave.

Ash wasn't a confident god. He knew how to make a planet spin and could do it just enough to avoid fucking the whole process, but he was no wizard at utopia. He preferred to let things play out.

"I like to see how things play out," Ash would always say. Love just thought he was lazy.

"Wouldn't it be easier to just tell them what to do?" Love suggested. She did have a point.

Ash and Love sat there staring at the phone booth. Where were they going to go? Their plan ended here. At least until that receiver rang. For now, it just hung silent and they were left to drink and think about what might have been.

They laughed and thought that maybe this was the end. This was the point. Kicking dust to create philosophical gradiose in the sand over and over again. For time infinite.

"I'll Write Your Name Through the Fire"
Shocking Blue (1969)

A hypnotic rhythm with melody, beats, crashes, and a lovely vocal line. Slightly slurred Dutch vocals draw you in and you're washed down the road by a circular guitar line woven in time with the syncopated rhythm section.

Well, we are all searching backwards in time. Even if we find a home or are eternally searching for one, it's just one of the things we are always reaching for.

A Psychedelic Pitch

Ace jogged down the middle of the sidewalk. He eyed the road, always watching for cars. Ace always jogged with his head down, but he glanced up every now and again to make sure he wouldn't trip and land on the pavement.

Ace felt his phone buzz once in his pocket. It was probably Thom, his fucking agent, trying to get hold of him. Ace didn't bother to check, he was tired of it.

Ace had done his time with lower division English football clubs. Three years at Luton Town, one at Grimsby, and another four before that at Notts County taught him everything he needed to know about jogging six days a week. Ace tried his best to keep match fit even if he was out of contract. He stopped, coughed, and wiped the sweat coming down his face. If only his agent could do his job.

Colors streaked across the sky, running parallel to the path Ace jogged. The leaves leaked purple colors that shifted into black, which then regenerated back into fresh leaves, lifted, and flew away like aimless birds. Ace dug into the pavement and ran harder. The sweat gathered on his forehead and he opened his eyes wider while shaking out his hair.

An old lady nodded at Ace, hoping he wouldn't jog straight into her.

Every stride on the pavement resembled a stroke in the community pool. The air thickened like gelatin as he jogged down the sidewalk.

At 32, Ace felt more like 52. A football contract had remained out of reach for the last thirteen months. His agent, Thom, would spin tall tales about some club in China or Hong Kong. He'd invite Ace out for a meeting at some bar. After three or four beers, he would always ask Ace to split the bill.

Most fullbacks found it to be a tough trade, especially in the states. And especially for a player like Ace, who most scouts would accurately pencil in as "slow." He knew how to motor, but couldn't keep pace with the kids. The kids always seemed to have that extra "gear."

Despite his limited gearbox, Ace could jog. Nobody could take that away from him. He had his hair too, which grew longer each day. Ace kept it in place with a thin band around his head. His ex-girlfriend thought he looked like Tymoshchuk. Not a bad compliment, Ace would always tell her. A Ukrainian superstar was not a bad guy to be compared to. Not bad at all.

Ace avoided the old lady. She moved to her left and almost fell into the street. She stared at Ace, but he looked down as he jogged. The same thing happened a few minutes later, with a teenager ditching out of the way of Ace's jogging. This time, the teenage girl laughed at him, the aging Englishman with his hair held off his forehead by a thin band wrapping around his head. Ace didn't mind the laughter, he didn't see it staring down at the ground.

Ace figured he was bound to get some stares when he left his brother's apartment. His jogging outfit consisted of a pair of snug jeans, a Millwall track-top, and a pair of worn tennis shoes. People seemed to look at Ace and wonder whether he was exercising or running away from the scene of a crime.

"Late again, Ace?" Brooks always laughed when Ace came in.

Brooks bartended at the Welsh Dragon and Ace was one of the few regulars at the joint. He always showed up sometime early in the afternoon or like today, 11:30am. Brooks would run through last night's sales, restock, and shoot the shit with Ace who provided the commentary. Whether Ace was waxing about his football adventures or singing some chant or teaching Brooks zonal marking, it was a bit of comic relief needed during the daytime at a bar.

"Who's playing today?" Brooks asked. He knew there must be a match. Ace only showed up this early for one reason.

"FA Cup. West Ham," Ace said.

"Well, you don't want to miss kick-off. The usual?"

Ace nodded. Brooks filled a pint and laid it on the bar for him. Ace did not make eye contact with Brooks, just stared at the TV screen and the full pint glass. Ace's phone buzzed again. Must have been Thom again. Too bad he couldn't just find Ace a club in Los Angeles. That way, he could jog here for a beer after training.

Ace's eyes were two big, black platters today. He wondered if Brooks could see this.

Tiny, Brooks' girlfriend, walked in. Smart, beautiful and tough. Ace thought Brooks was a lucky man.

"Tarragon," Ace laughed. That was his name for Tiny.

"What's on the TV today, you English fuck?" Tarragon shot back. That was her name for Ace. They were even.

"Nothing you care about. Just a few blokes skipping on the grass," Ace said.

"So why do you care then?"

"Why do I what?" Ace wasn't paying attention to Tarragon.

"Never mind."

Ace slipped away again.

When the pace of the match slowed a bit, he explained it to Brooks and Tarragon. It wasn't just the FA Cup, but the FA Cup Final. West Ham surprised everyone, but their opponent was Manchester City, Oil City F.C. The rich kids vs. the bullies.

"Where are they both from?" Tarragon liked Ace's build-up.

"Manchester and London."

Ace had a way with words that only got better once the pint kicked in. He then started talking about the formations, the influence of money in the game, philosophy. Long Ball. Tiki-Taka. Withdrawn forwards. 6-4-0. 4-4-2. 4-4-2 Diamond. 4-5-1. The W. The V. Sweeper Keepers. Total Football. Dukla Prague. Nottingham Forest. Brooks and Tarragon gave each other a look. They had worked in bars long enough to know that there must be some truth to Ace's tales, but most of this was drunken bullshit.

Ace continued on like this for a long time, spewing knowledge that Tiny and Brooks didn't think he possessed. Ace's accent loaned credibility to his stories, even if it was more East London than Buckingham Palace.

Tarragon and Brooks seemed surprised, because Ace wasn't slipping away today. Brooks always gave Ace a 50% chance of settling up in full. Ace had started coming around for the past few months, something about staying with his brother who was a lawyer for a movie producer in Century City. Wasn't everybody's brother? They asked Ace about why he didn't play anymore, but had never gotten more than a few words about tryouts, his lousy agent, and Erik Wynalda.

"And that's why I'd never be taken. The league is a single entity system. Unfair to the players, especially a bloke like me. Plus, it's all possession and, fuck the long ball," Ace made an airplane gesture with his left taking off like an airplane, using his right arm as the runway. His gesture was meant to say "To the fucking moon." Brooks and Tarragon had no idea what Ace was talking about.

Ace could see that Tarragon noticed his eyes. They were usually red and watery, but today resembled gothic dinner plates. Large and black and wide.

"What are you on?"

"Oh man," Ace laughed. The game was about to start, so it was easier to reach into his pocket and pull out a small handful of mushrooms. Tarragon and Brooks laughed, which caused Ace to laugh even harder.

"Give us some." Tarragon asked, sort of.

"Ok, do you have any hot sauce?"

"Yeah, I think so. Brooks, we have any hot sauce?"

"Yeah, what for?"

"What do you think?"

Brooks pulled out the bottle of hot sauce and they both poured a healthy amount of it into their mouths as they ate the mushrooms raw. Their mouths burned, but that only helped mask the taste of shit.

The game had kicked off.

For the first twenty minutes or so, it was the same drab affair Brooks and Tarragon had imagined it would be. They were entertained by Ace.

"Fuck."

"C'mon, you fucking wanker."

"For fuck's sakes."

"Jesus fucking Christ."

And on Ace went.

By right around the 28th minute, it kicked in. For all three of them, but with Ace ahead of the rest. Color filled the bar. The game's rays bounced off the mirror in the back and shimmied in their pint glasses.

Tarragon saw the magic on the field. The players passing, anticipating and improvising. She didn't get why the guy in yellow would raise his flag, but figured the players must have done something wrong. They all started running back up the field. It was constant movement, a flow of anticipation and the ball was being shared by all.

Brooks stared at Tarragon. He could see her eyes darting rapidly at the screen as he played behind the bar. He picked up a rag and pretended to wipe away something and saw the light of the television reflect through each of the liquor bottles. He turned around and saw a bunch of guys moving about. The colors of their jerseys melded with the green of the grass into a swirl. He looked back at Tarragon.

Ace studied the players, deep in a meditation, with a few fucks thrown in for good measure. He looked at the players, wishing he was there. He could feel the short grass, smell the gray overcast sky and hear the chants of the crowd. Of course, his past play never filled stadiums, but he'd had a good run. Watching these games was less of an exercise for Ace and more of a dream-like trance. He muttered softly to himself. That was just for him, the fucks were for everyone else.

He looked at his phone. Two missed messages from Thom, but still no call from his brother. He felt like a boat, cut loose and drifting further from shore. Well, at least the bar was providing him a safe harbor for the moment.

At half-time, they all huddled around the tap and decided what music to put on. They talked and talked more. Nothing felt quite right. It was too quiet with the only noise being cars driving by on the street.

They chose a tune and continued on. Brooks went out for a smoke. Tarragon went to stare in a mirror in the bathroom and Ace stayed where he was, looking at his reflection in the mirror behind the bar.

The group rejoined for the second half. Back together again. This time, it was more jovial. West Ham had slotted one in the right corner of the goal and was up 1-0.

Ace shouted, "About fucking time." He made them all laugh.

The rest of the game followed a similar pattern of fucks and laughter, with Brooks pouring a couple of pints to keep it all loose enough.

The game ended quicker than Tarragon or Brooks thought it would. But there they were. 1-0 West Ham United. Ace smiled.

He finished his third beer.

"Hey, Brooks. I'm good for it. My brother said he has a gig for me this week."

"Yeah, we can call it even with the mushrooms."

They all started to laugh again and Ace gave him a handshake, waved at Tarragon.

Ace walked out the door and into the Southern California sun. He picked up the phone and dialed Thom. Even if he was a shitty agent, they could have a few laughs and split a pitcher or two. No answer.

"Fuck 'em," Ace told himself. It was hot outside and he had a good buzz going from the beers and mushrooms. He put in his headphones and started to jog back home.

"Shifting Sands"
West Coast Pop Art Experimental Band (1967)

A slice of California heaven. Bouncy psychedelia from start to finish, with an almost-sinister underbelly. The perfect soundtrack for sunshine, mushrooms, and whatever else comes along.

It's magical when music becomes liquid, running down the speakers and into the listener's ears. Closing your eyes, visions of ever-changing eternity can be held again and again, long after the record clips at the end of the two or three minutes.

Pure huckster or pure black magic, it doesn't really matter. This song could be thought of as a transcendental slice, but think too hard or too long and it spills through our fingers to the earth below.

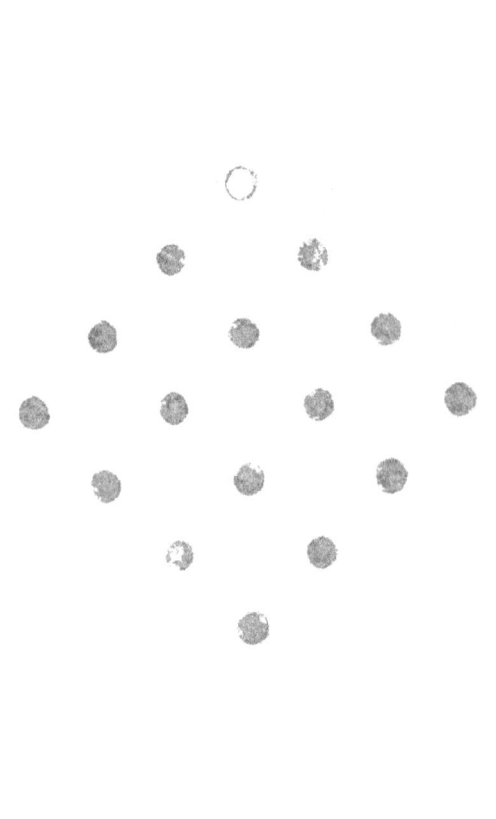

Nines

Today felt special, August told himself as he drove Rose down the road. Working in the city had kept them from really getting out to the fresh air. The Douglas Firs and the big sky. Sure, they had their bonfires in their backyard, but that was mostly just an excuse to get stoned outside.

Today was different. Their Volvo rumbled down the road and August didn't mind the fast cars when they whipped by him. He enjoyed the sun's angled rays between the trees. Light shined differently in the autumn.

He looked over at Rose. She wore a pair of heart-shaped sunglasses. The sun streamed through the window into her side of the car. She gazed away from him, her dreams spilt out into the woods on the side of the road.

They were going to the Gray Dog Crest trailhead, a secluded loop in the mountains. August's dad had taken he and his brother there when they were kids. Rose liked it too. They used to do the hike a couple of times a year, but they didn't go last year. Why didn't they? He didn't know.

August knew that the turn up to the trailhead was in two miles or so. After that, he would continue down an abandoned logging road. First, though, he wanted to stop for supplies: a couple of cheap cans of beer and a granola bar.

He pulled over in the parking lot of the Gold Rush General Store. The store seemed quaint. It had an old wooden exterior and a carved, smiling black bear out front to greet customers.

"I'll be right back," August said to Rose.

He heard two middle-aged men talking about something when he walked in. He pretended not to listen as he shopped. The radio crackled with Top 40.

"Well, somebody said they saw him."

"Old Man Nine?"

"Yeah."

"No fucking way."

"They say he's still up there." August noticed out of the corner of his eye that one of the guys pointed in the general direction of Gray Dog Crest.

"Yeah, my ass."

"Your ass? That'll be the only thing that'll save you if you run into Nine."

"No running into Nine. He doesn't really—" He stopped mid-sentence. The guys turned to August, who placed two cans of cheap beer and a raisin granola bar on the counter.

"Who's Nine?" August asked.

"Nine visits the hills around here. Right up near Gray Dog Crest."

"What do you mean *visits*?"

The two men smiled and started in about the local vortex of supernatural activity. They handed him a pamphlet. It included a 10% off coupon for the vortex visitor center in town. August glanced at the pamphlet and saw that it cost $5 each to go inside and visit the natural prism.

August thanked the men and hopped in the car.

"What took you so long?" Rose asked.

"Nothing, couple of guys told me about Nine."

"Who?"

"Oh, just a story about someone or something around here, not too sure. Sounded funny."

Everything felt eternal.

The sun split the sky and filled the horizon with reds, pinks and purples. This light spilt through the window as he rose in the morning. The house he lived in was more a shelter than a home, but it was his. Always was. One concrete room and bare walls. A single mattress on the floor. The wood stove, a small sink with no running water, a rug for his dog, a small pile of clothes and a record player, battery-powered, with one record and a tattered sleeve. Beside the bed were his brown boots, caked with mud and dirt. Propped up against the wall was his rifle. His hat hung from the wall on a single nail. The hat was wide-brimmed and floppy. It fit him snug.

Outside there was a small bathroom shack and about fifteen feet from that was the storage shed, holding canned goods, sacks of grain, and batteries for the record player.

This morning, he walked outside and grabbed two pieces of the wood he split last week. He added them to the fire and opened the flue to get the sucker going.

It didn't take long for the wood to catch. He placed a metal percolator with ground coffee and hot water on top. It brewed in a few minutes. The bitterness of the coffee didn't seem to bother him. The coffee had been ground ages ago so it lacked the oils and flavor that most people enjoy. To him, it was coffee.

He cooked one egg in his one pan and complemented it with one piece of hard, stale bread. That was enough to get him through the morning. The dog barked. She seemed to agree. He dropped one piece of the hard, stale bread on the floor for her. She ate a rabbit last night anyway, so she could find herself a meal this morning too, he told himself.

He stood up and placed his hat on his head. He grabbed his gun, put it over his shoulder and closed the door behind him. Walking outside, he knew it was a day mostly the same as it always was, but something was a little different. The little difference was how he could tell the days apart.

He looked around. The view from the top of the crest would stun anyone this time of year. The rays of sunshine bent in autumn like no other time. It mixed the brown, dead leaves into a strange brew.

The trail down from the crest was one person wide. Narrow and windy, just like it had always been. He peered ahead through the scope of his wooden rifle. Never know who you'd run into up in these hills.

Lucky for him, there was just the one trail. One way in and one way out. The path narrowed up here, but widened a bit towards the base.

Every day was the same for him. Walking up and down and around the same crest with his dog.

All of the sudden, his dog ran ahead barking at something. Or she ran ahead and barked at nothing. He didn't know for sure, dogs were mysterious in that way.

August and Rose started up the trail with the two cans of cheap beer and the granola bar. Their jackets would keep them warm enough and the trail up to the crest was short enough that they would soon be home anyway, or at least back at the car.

They had parked on the side of the road. No one came up here anymore. The seclusion was sweet.

Starting up the trail, the path was wide, maybe three or four feet, but soon narrowed as the trail wound up and up towards the crest.

August and Rose walked on in silence. Even though it was only 3pm, the sunshine of the day gave way to the darkness of tree cover. The shadows and light took turns around each bend.

Maybe twenty minutes longer and they'd be up there.

They walked around one turn and then another. August grabbed the granola bar. He took a bite and tossed it to Rose. She didn't catch it.

The granola bar made a soft landing in the brush. August and Rose looked at each other, half-smiling and half-anxious.

Rose tiptoed into the brush. She was not going to let a half-eaten granola bar go to waste.

His dog would not stop barking. He was pretty sure nothing was out there, but why was she so persistent?

He adjusted the brim on his hat, pulled up his rifle and adjusted it. The scope was a little fuzzy so he couldn't see anything that far away. He felt a cold breeze drift right through him. The autumn always felt like that. Warmth in the sun and cold in the shadows, with a few drafts holding the in-between.

She was still barking, maybe twenty yards ahead, but now she was headed into the brush. She found something.

He walked faster. Must be a rabbit. He was now walking faster than he walked every day. He thought he knew everything out here. He walked past the brush and she was still barking, this time off the trail. Only a few more minutes and he'd be down at the bottom of the road anyway. It was an old logging road, hadn't been used for years. Sometimes there were days or even weeks without a car on it. He couldn't remember the last time he had seen anyone on the trail, let alone driving on that road.

What was she barking at? He didn't like the sound of it. He clutched his rifle and pulled down his hat. He also didn't like when he found campers—after all, this was his trail.

He went into the brush after her, but before he stepped off the trail, she came running back. He wished she could tell him what she was barking at.

They started down the trail again.

Another 10 minutes and they were at the base of the trail. They continued to walk out towards the main highway. He liked living alone, but everybody needs supplies. And everybody needs to see someone else from time to time.

After another fifteen minutes, he came up to the Gold Rush General Store. He wondered how long this place had been around. Seemed like forever. How did they make money if nobody ever came in? They wouldn't even let him take his dog in.

He told her "stay" as he entered the store. She always did.

There were two old guys behind the counter and the radio was crackling.

"Did I ever tell you the story?" one of the guys said.

"Of course, you have." The other said. "Are you still talking about Ten and Eleven?"

He placed two cans of beer on the counter and looked at his watch. 11:00am was never too early to start drinking.

He put down a few dollars and smiled at the two old-timers behind the counter. They smiled back and placed the change in his hand.

He walked out with the two beers in a brown paper sack, whistled to his dog and they started their journey back up to Grey Dog Crest.

"Hiway Man"
Blue Cheer (1971)

A solid rocker from the heaviest of San Francisco heavies. Sure, not a classic, but they'd shaken their Summertime Blues by the time they tied this one on. Gary Yoder injecting a bit of Northern California brown grass into it.

Envision driving from Williams to San Francisco, before you really hit the traffic. Driving out into those golden hills off the highway, somewhere northeast of Vacaville, before hitting the bright lights and the big city.

An apt, lonesome tune about people taking what they want and others only taking what they can get...

Mercury Rand

The butler saw flashing lights again. They snuck out from underneath the prince's bedroom door. A leak of blues, reds, pinks, and oranges. They ran down the floor and spilled out on the stairs leading from his room.

"If colors run, am I standing still?" The butler thought.

What a strange, strange prince. The butler knew this, but it needed repeating.

The butler was not alone. Everyone else had the same thoughts about the man he served and his family, the Rands. This upright, uptight family somehow bore a son that resembled nothing the family stood for. This family balanced the ceremonial powers of monarchy with ease and awareness, even if their principality took up no more than a few anonymous valleys in the mountains of Europe.

The Rands stood like that one tall tree in every neighborhood that has been there for too long. The tree begins to rot from the inside as its limbs lose their luster and its foliage barely registers autumn. The Rands covered in the moss of an earlier age. No one told them that things were different. It just didn't seem right to have to tell them. The Rands must have known they were rotting, right?

The Rands never grabbed more land or power than they had to. They stayed in a sustained period of mediocre wealth throughout the years. They shuffled alongside those with more lofty pursuits. While other families rose and fell, the Rands kept bobbing along.

Prince Rand was the strangest fucking thing on either side of this millennium, so he was the best candidate to usher in a new age of royals with a lowercase r.

They were known primarily for three things: Kindness, Honor and Manners. While it once was a destination for gallantry and splendor, their land was now tucked away as a rump state. Not well known in history books and only a footnote in online encyclopedias, the Rands could rest easy knowing that they pushed for a more buttoned-up and starched society. A society where the men spoke in measured tones and women wielded enough influence to keep everything just right.

That's what made Prince Rand all the stranger. No one saw Mercury for long, but when they did, it was not mediocre. Tall, beautiful and slender, his stark look was an extreme for these small European valleys populated with brown-haired people of normal proportions.

There were plenty of rumors about Mercury. He raced down the streets with black boots, tight jeans and a long, loose tangle of hair. Some talked about seeing Mercury watching bands at underground clubs. Nobody seemed to get a clear look at him, but they always swore it was his shadow moving through the alleys after the bars let out, with a good-looking lady or boy on his arm. Others swore he wore a black, floppy hat that tied loosely under his chin. Other people talked about a drink he bought them or a joint he'd shared with them. There were a lot of stories, but the younger kids in town loved them, as they would any rich, teenaged mystery.

But could anyone say what Mercury looked like? The butler thought.

The Butler had raised Mercury from the time he was a little kid. The round-faced boy had grown lean and wiry. The Butler felt something was off with Mercury. He was reminded of one of those wires left dangling in the attic, just waiting for a spark to ignite and catch fire. This fire would bring the Rands down. The Butler felt it was his duty to save them.

Even as a child, Prince Mercury screamed and ran like a madman down the halls. His little toys were always lined up in antiquated formations in nooks around the property. Typical rich kid shit, the Butler knew. The way he would look at the Butler with piercing, hollow eyes. He used to see Mercury every day, but now it had been weeks without anything but an empty plate and a faraway voice.

Mercury was 18 and had fostered a world all his own. The Butler never met his friends, but they would slink like shadows up the back stairway. Just a couple of weeks ago, he almost ran straight into Mercury, who brushed past him and barely mumbled a greeting. His parents did nothing, of course. The Butler wondered if they even noticed or if they just preferred to look the other way.

The Butler delivered Mercury the same food every night. Mashed potatoes. Plain with butter neatly placed on the right side of the plate. He left the mashed potatoes outside the door. Every night, the sounds wailed against the wooden door.

Every night was the same. Not exactly the same, as the liquid colors changed and the abrasive noises vibrated at different frequencies. Still, the Butler had his routine with Mercury.

He always knocked three times. Each knock got progressively louder. knock. Knock. KNOCK!

As the Butler shuffled away each night, he heard Mercury open the door. The music rushed out, like heat into a cold room. Like light into the vacuum of space. Every night sounded like noise to the Butler.

What the hell was it with those mashed potatoes? The Butler just shook his head and said out loud to himself.

Nobody really knew, but everybody had their own story about strange Prince Mercury. Whispers were passed. Tales woven.

Stories about Prince Mercury, the madman. Nightly rituals of alchemy. Another tale told about how Prince Mercury was secretly just dumb and would roll around smearing the mashed potatoes in his hair. Some about famous bands that recorded secret albums in the Rand mansion. Some even swore you could hear lips smacking as they spooned mashed potatoes way, way down in the mix. Mashed potatoes mixed with the blood of babies.

Sexual perversions too. Mashed potatoes used in all sorts of sensual ways. Perverts and oddballs must have been Mercury's company. Or so the stories went. People loved to hear about fucking. The weirder, the more depraved, the better.

Every morning, the plate was empty. The lights were done seeping from the door and only gray light remained.

The next night, the colors were brighter and the noise even louder. It ground deep into the Butler's mind.

Can you taste music? the Butler thought to himself.

The sounds were so odd that he swore he tasted their tones on his tongue. The music wasn't shoved in his mouth, but placed there like a drop of acid on a piece of dry wood. One or two drops burned a hole and altered the Butler's mind.

He had been doing this for years. How long had the Butler tasted Mercury's music? Was it just tonight or all along?

He put down the mashed potatoes and put his ear up against the door.

He looked down at the colors still running across the wooden floors. The colors and sounds joined like a waterfall and ran over the stairs.

He went to the stairs to see where the colors went. Nowhere. The colors were gone. Like chasing fog. He turned around and could see the colors seeping out from underneath the door and running toward him all over again.

He turned around to look at the stairs and then back at the door. Walking back and forth, he did this for what seemed like an hour. Then all of sudden, before he could capture the colors—WHAM! The door shut. At the base of the door was the empty plate. Clean. The mashed potatoes were gone.

Goddamnit. The prince had done it again, but this time the Butler broke. These fucking mashed potatoes, he thought to himself.

What was he doing with them?

Sometimes it sounded like a strummed balalaika. Other times it was a breeze of cold air that hugged him. Still, there was no end to the strangeness.

This was the last night, the Butler assured himself. He put the empty, clean plate next to the stairs and straightened his uniform to appear most presentable. He cleared his throat and marched back to Mercury's door.

He knocked three times, each one loud. KNOCK. KNOCK. KNOCK. No answer. He knocked again. KNOCK. KNOCK. KNOCK. Still no answer, but the music still spilled out with the colors under the door.

The Butler checked the handle. It was unlocked. He flung the door open and rushed inside. Immediately, the colors blinded him and the noise enveloped him. The Butler held his hand up to his face. He looked around and around, but could not find the prince.

The music felt so powerful it almost knocked him to the ground. The Butler heard the door close behind him, so he spun around, but saw nothing. He could hear someone's lips smacking as they ate, but it sounded like it was at the other end of the room. The Butler hurried to that end of the room, but the lights cut out and the sound vanished. It was dark. Too dark to see whether he was at one end of the room or the other. Too dark to find his way out.

The Butler thought about time for what could've been a long time. Or what could've been just a few moments, he wasn't sure. It's tough with just the mind to keep the clock.

"How long have I been in here?"

"Why can't I find the walls?"

"Where is the door?"

"Where am I?"

Those questions and the question of time swirled around and around.

The Butler had almost answered the first question when the liquid lights burst on and the sounds ground back into his brain. He got up to find his way out, but before he took a step forward, he heard three knocks on the other side of the door, each one progressively louder. knock. Knock. KNOCK.

"Robert Montgomery"
Love (1969)

Weirdness from the ins and outs. The guitar riff rings right through the speakers with drums that bash and crash. Listen closely to the ups and downs and learn how envy is just the same as love.

The stops-and-starts come out like multi-colored coils wrapping around and around. Heavy thoughts that make you understand that the times are just as weird as you think they are. And you are as out there as the times. Heavy thoughts indeed.

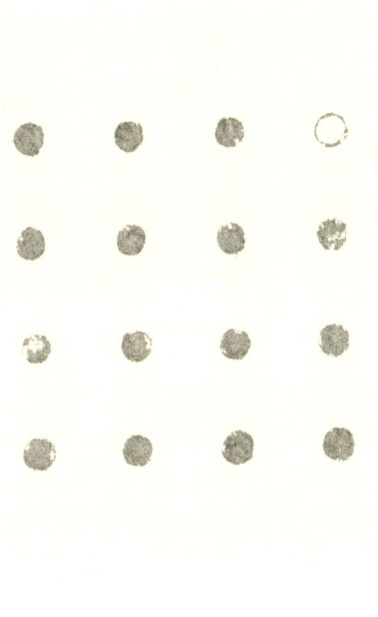

A Strange Red

Red does the strangest fucking things when he's high. Some may ask, "But doesn't everyone?" Maybe, but Red is a rare bird. Multicolored strands hold his feeble mind together.

Red wears his black jeans faded and tight. Black sneakers on his feet grimed with the filth from a spring shower. His jean jacket frayed at the cuffs and adorned with a button of his favorite band and some obsolete beer brand. The jacket fit a little tighter at 28 than when he had bought it secondhand at 22. The jacket and Red work together. Friends do that sort of thing.

Last week, Red remembered standing in the rain in red underwear and a straw hat, but without his black sneakers and tight, frayed jean jacket. Red talked with squirrels that scurried away. He leered at 80-year-old men last night, with his black sneakers and tight, frayed jean jacket. Just to give it back to them.

How did he get to this party? Twenty or so people talking, listening to a record player spin as they all ask the same thing. People drinking, laughing, and debating while Red spins around mumbling. Some stranger hears a story from Red about the Sick Man of Europe and the British cavalry movements to repel Ottoman forces. Or was it more about the Dardanelles? Or the ups and downs of Bismarck's foreign policy as it related to current fiscal policy? The stranger smiles at Red, nothing to worry about.

Some people just have *it* and Red is not one of them. Despite the lack of *it*, he prances on with his queer anecdotes on late 1800s economic schemes. Lisa, a woman who Red does not know, notices foam forming on his lips.

Red's eyes slant and roll to the side and just like that he is gone. Off to the bathroom.

"Who invited *him*?" Lisa asks to no one in particular.

Some guy with a beard shrugs his shoulders. He turned to the guy next him. And then that guy turns to the next stranger and on and on and on.

Red does the strangest fucking things when he's high. This is one of them. Jacking off in some stranger's bathroom at some other stranger's party while even more strangers roll their eyes at the stranger in front of them. One stranger near the front of the line starts pounding on the door.

The sound startles Red. Not enough to stop, but the pounding jars his fantasy. Like a child shaking a snow globe, his mind buzzes in white flakes. He forgets all about the stranger at the door and continues thinking of Dawn in his free hand.

Is Red a pervert? Probably. But who needs to judge Red? That's not really the point. Poor Red, he tries to be discreet. Jacking off at some stranger's party seemed familiar and, well, at least he wasn't making much of a mess. And Red remembers to turn on the ceiling fan to help with the acoustics.

How did Red get here? He ran into the bathroom in the back of the apartment to take a piss. He also wanted a bump or two of the coke that he had in his pocket. Red's not an animal, sneaking off to beat his meat at a party. He took a piss first, much needed after the beers he drank at the bar across the street from his place a couple of hours ago.

"I probably should have eaten something," Red says to himself. He'd had a couple of stone wheat crackers with hummus, but that's not quite a meal.

He looks down at his frayed jean jacket and remembers he still has that black marker in his pocket. He enjoys writing in large black letters. He always writes what he is thinking.

Smiling, he looks in the mirror at his black ink scrawlings:

...What is love...who...is love...

It is something our minds know...in between

Our minds can feel love...in reverse

That's enough for now, Red thinks. The balance of his mind always depends on what's going in it. Red carries a heavy load. The one thing he couldn't seem to squeeze in, though, is Dawn.

He thinks about their last night together. A few weeks ago on a Tuesday or Wednesday. A mid-week dinner out at a regular place. Nothing too special, except it meant something to Red. They ordered a $24 bottle of red table wine. It was a blend of grapes from California. They drank it over two courses and ordered another bottle. Red likes dates, especially when he knows what to expect. He also likes to talk about wine. Almost as much as he likes to talk about pashas, janissaries, and forgotten empires.

Dawn is a girl to Red. One to hold on to. The one to grow old with, have kids with, fight while washing dishes with and all of that same shit. Dawn's never going to do this, but Red wants to keep that fantasy. The girl outstretched, just out of reach from his hand. Red's hand shakes a little, either from the coke, the blue pills, or the beer. Or all three.

Red and Dawn met a few weeks earlier. She was walking with her face staring at the sidewalk when Red walked (SLAM!) right into her. He laughed, she did too. They had a few good weeks, but Dawn moved on to another party on the other side of town. Red tried sending cryptic text messages earlier today, but no response from Dawn. He only sees the words "READ" right below his messages. Why does Red wait to send his messages until he's too far gone?

It just freaks everyone out. Red knows the late morning is best for everything.

But, back to the bathroom, Red, his black sneakers, and frayed jean jacket grasping for lucidity. Not many people think about Red doing what he's doing now. It's one of those things nobody wants to talk about.

But here's Red taking out the garbage behind a hollow wooden door while a line of strangers wait. The strangers tap their feet and check their phones. Have these strangers paid their cellphone bills yet? The strangers roll their eyes and do everything short of confronting Red. One stranger thinks he's tying one off. Another stranger assumes that Red is taking a shit.

Inside Red's mind, he's fucking that blonde barista he gets his 20-ounce black coffee from most mornings. The vision shakes a little. Red has to focus. FOCUS. Red's bending her over the bathroom sink. The blonde looks back, angry that she's in some stranger's bathroom, bent over and fucked like a doll in some man's fantasy.

Red draws a breath and thinks deeply about this fantasy and where it started. Talking with her after drinking his black coffee one morning? No, the fantasy would be better if it is later in the day. Nobody has sex with strangers in the morning unless they are awake from the night before or really into that sort of thing.

Johnny, the stranger at the front of the line, is about to piss himself. Too much beer for him. He stares as he has for the last ten minutes. This stranger tries to think about anything other than taking a piss. Not one of the strangers, not even Johnny, imagines that Red is cleaning the cat's litter box.

Yes, Red is taking out the garbage behind the closed door. His free hand stretches out towards the mirror and goes into it and back out again.

Red thinks paying his cellphone bill takes too long after a few bumps of coke. Red needs more. He adds old books, antiquities, Victorian women, Archduke Ferdinand, the Hapsburgs, Bismarck, a Polish queen and a half-spoiled ham to the bent-over, fucked blonde.

All of the sudden Red rushes towards the end. The blood flows to his mind. His arms shake a little and feel like they are walking to the door by themselves. For one second...two seconds...he looks in the mirror and swears he sees ЯƎᗡ smiling back.

Red's garbage bill payment deposits in the toilet paper. He drops it in and flushes. Red takes his keys out. One last bump to breeze him up and out of the doldrums.

Ziippp. Red opens the door.

"Hey man, what are you doing in there?", Johnny, the stranger, asks.

"Huh?" Red replies.

Johnny, rolls his eyes and Red keeps walking down the hall, out through the main room, out the front door and into the street.

It's dark at night. He's coming down, but he's still just high enough to text Dawn.

"*Mona Bone Jakon*"
Cat Stevens (1970)

A soundtrack fitting for trashcan fantasies. A balance of beauty, acoustics and warbled vocals. An eerie tune by this young, almost superstar singer. Dive headfirst into his smut dumpster. This song is a treat for a dark room, a dark night, or a dark rainy day.

This is not the Wild World you've come to associate with the 1970s stalwart. With equal hints of desperation and danger, it urges you to dream about swimming inside your mind on the wrong side of town.

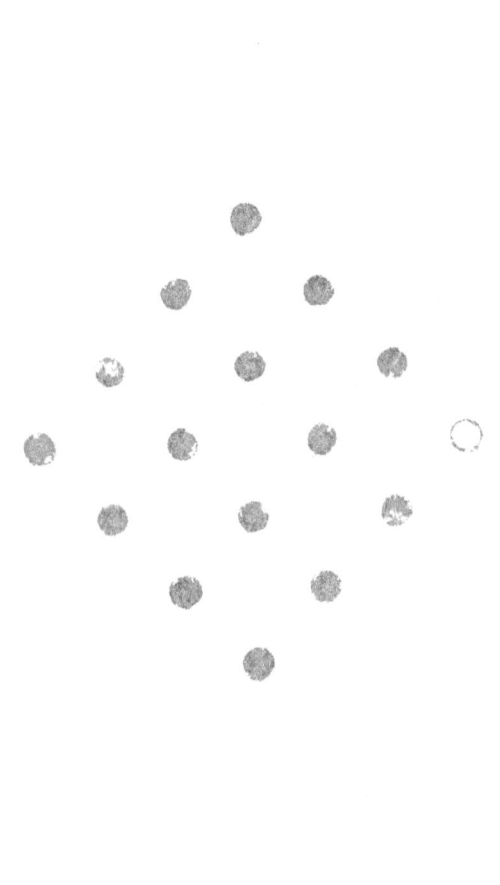

Wide Time

Imagine two people sitting on a bench. They're wrapped together in a thick fog. It could really be any cloudy, coastal city. San Francisco? Too easy. Cardiff? Too accented. Agadir? Too tedious. Doesn't matter anyway. Here they are, in the middle of a city. They are wrapped tight together in the middle of a fog bank.

Together, Bullet and Lace.

The fog dense and thick around his hair. Turning left, shadows and the rumble of waves whisper to him. Turning right, Lace talks with more familiar words.

How did they get here? Bullet wonders. Maybe ask the waves. They always come in packs.

Bullet remembers coming down near the beach for a coffee and stopping on this bench for a cigarette. He should stop smoking one of these days. He won't, but he should. It's a routine and Bullet feels that routines are meant to be kept.

Lace takes the same walk every morning. She works the night shift at a mediocre Italian restaurant. She wakes up early in the morning because she likes joining the world of the living. Waking up with the businessmen and bakers makes last night's complaints of overcooked pasta tolerable. Lace thinks a little too much this morning. She is still thinking while she sits with Bullet, both of them wrapped together tightly in a fog bank.

Lace puts out her finger. She remembers seeing her fingers pass in and out of the cloud. Bullet knows that she struck up the conversation with him. Lace tries to convince Bullet that it was him dropping his lit cigarette that made the introduction.

Either way, here they are. Talking to you, me and the in-between. They sit there wrapped together in a fog bank.

"And that's why we're here. You and me. And that too," Lace points to a pile of driftwood. Bullet thinks it's funny that wood so close to the sea is always so dry. They talk about it for a while.

At this very moment, neither is in the world around them. Not in the least. Minutes, hours, and days can pass within the time of another story. Worlds live and die between them and around them. The sun rises and sets a million times after each story they share, wrapped together in a fog bank.

At this very moment, no time passes at all. The fog hangs frozen and the breath which Bullet uses to talk about his love for Rhone wines never actually leaves his throat. Lace's sneeze hangs in her nose forever. This would make anyone uncomfortable.

All the while, people are walking by in their own everlasting fog bank during this eternity of moment. Clouds streak barenaked like the ghosts people see when they close their eyes. Nobody talks to strangers, so Bullet and Lace don't have to worry about being interrupted.

They feel nothing, but time stretches, bending at this very moment. They talk about kings, queens, and earls. Bullet lights another cigarette and she tells him that she wishes she had a drink. Him too. They decide that they will take the morning to dream up the past and study the future. It's better that way around. It makes more sense.

Bullet thinks that they are speaking a completely different language. It sounds like English to him, but sort of different. Sort of strong, like maybe she has an accent he does not remember. He did just meet her, after all. Lace thinks he sounds familiar, but is he from England?

That's it, Bullet thinks to himself. It must be Welsh. They are speaking Welsh. Or do they call it Gaelic? Something like that. Lace knows it's not that. She tells him that she was teased in school.

"Whales. What's wrong with an extra 'h' from time to time? I would probably go there, but not now. Sounds boring," Lace tells him.

Bullet only knows that there are a lot of miners there. His hands are much too soft for that line of work, except for the calluses on his fingers.

Holding out his hand, Bullet shows Lace his picking hand and why he is destined for more. She smiles and tells him that she'd love to cook in her own restaurant.

They talk longer and expand on their dreams. They talk about the generations after, tying dreams to each other to see if they would take off and fly. They talk more as they are wrapped together in a fog bank.

"But what does their flag look like," Lace says. She racks her mind to come up with something, remembering that geography was a course that never stimulated her brain. She tells Bullet how it is all just colors and lines on paper. Bullet tells her that there are a lot of important things that those colors and lines mean. Lace shrugs her shoulders.

They talk about space. They talk about the pictures they see of colorful galaxies with pinwheel planets and other destinations that have mouths eating all the stars they can over millions of years. Lace tells Bullet that those pictures are just art and colored for effect. The colors must be there to make us feel. Bullet and Lace continue down this path as they sit, wrapped together in a fog bank.

"I think it has a dragon," Bullet answers. "Ohhh," they both say, wrapped together in a fog bank.

Lace thinks that Bullet must be in college. That's the only place where you need this type of knowledge. She imagines college as ivy-covered buildings and heated discussions about flags, Faulkner and fungibility. But Bullet knows this because he used to study every nation's flag when he was a kid. Wales' makes Bullet think of a time when men walked around in thick metal armor and died young.

These flags stick with him through all the millennia, through all the moments. Tucked away, just for him to tell Lace.

"Well, not *my* restaurant, I don't own it. But you know what I mean," Lace talks about her job. Bullet thinks Lace must be a talented woman with knowledge of balance, palettes, and textures. He thinks this while they sit talking, wrapped together in a fog bank.

Sometimes Bullet and Lace talk with their mouths open, eyes looking at one another. Other times, she starts to wander, looking at one of the many birds scavenging at the edge of the fog bank. They talk about dreams of the future and what things could be like if they stayed here, wrapped together forever or even for just one more instant.

Lace's chestnut hair and intimate knowledge of saffron and other spices reminds Bullet of a dream he had where he traveled to Zanzibar with his parents. Bullet tells Lace about his record collection and Lace remembers her parents dancing at a concert when she was little.

On it goes, then back again. The words meander like a slow river with many bends. It leads them into a deep pool and empties out. They repeat this all over again. As they talk, the years lay out in front of them. Bullet's hair goes gray. Lace's cheeks tighten against her face. They both look good to each other as they sit aging, wrapped together in a fog bank.

They practice their farewells to one another.

Hellos are easy, but goodbyes are always a little tougher. Looking deeply into each other's eyes, Bullet tells Lace about the beauty of absence. Lace teaches Bullet about the understated brilliance of forever. Bullet and Lace carry on. They talk in languages lost and share cigarettes, wrapped together in a fog bank.

Just as Bullet's last words about an Abyssinian King hit Lace's ears, sunshine cuts the fog bank in two. The clouds lift and, in a few minutes, the sunny day brings an end to this foreverness.

The light hits Bullet's face and starts to blind Lace's eyes. They try to shield their eyes and carry on, but this doesn't last for long. They get up to leave and walk away on different paths. They forget to recite the goodbyes they have spent the past decades practicing together as they were wrapped in a fog bank. Practicing over and over again. Just for this moment. Bullet and Lace fade into the sunshine.

"Sand and Foam"
Donovan (1967)

A moment is a vexing object to catch. Once you have it, you look down and it is gone. When you try to remember, it is ever-moving backwards, or so it seems. This song is hypnotic and ever-present on a journey to a sun-filled land with crashing waves, crawling ants, microscopic beings, surfacing submarines, and phosphorus.

Across the landscape, the moments stay the same and the guitar picking floats above, providing a lush backdrop for contemplation.

Whether it is a memory of sunshine, a rainstorm, or a blizzard, imagine a beautiful statement about moments big, small, long or short. It's not the length of time, but the width that really matters.

So It Goes, Again

*"Some have hope. Some have dope.
Some have the in-between."*

Hawk didn't remember writing that line, but he must have at some point. The ink and paper couldn't have done it themselves. Maybe it was yesterday? Maybe the oblivions. Who really cared? His dog looked up at him, with one eye closed and the other half-open, staring at him. He sensed all the bullshit Hawk wrote with his pen. He knew.

He made more notes in his notebook. The notebook was black with a wide white stripe crossing diagonally from the upper left to the lower right. A faded red square on the back. Hawk didn't know where the square came from or where the notebook itself was sold. But he always had one in this room. He locked away the notebook when he was gone, but had it in view when he was by himself.

Hawk looked at the clock. 5:45pm. The darkness crept into the room at least ten minutes early. Someone dimmed the lights on the day.

The room was silent. Don shook his ears and Hawk petted his back. He stood up. It had been a long day. Full of thoughts. He flipped the record. The B-side played at medium volume. He didn't want it too loud to disturb his neighbors, but just loud enough so he could hear the crackle of the record as it started to flow out the speakers.

Hawk fixed himself with a clean spoon, a clean needle, and a little bit of light on a darkening day. A smile crossed his face.

This smile was the first spray of a cresting wave that washed over him. The sound wiggling his body, shaking him and running down his face.

Whuuummppffff.

Blood poured into his head, to the point where he lost a little of himself. The sound faded around him, just loud enough. The lights held steady, but flickered in his mind. His wide-open eyes blinked with a third eyelid. Closed, opened, closed and opened again.

Don stretched out his legs to get comfortable on the hardwood floor. Don didn't mind this room, but he hated the floors, especially when he rolled just right. It could feel like sandpaper on his coat. He wished that Hawk would do something about it, do something other than stare at the ceiling or write in his notebook or stare at the spinning record player.

The music swirled around the room. Hawk was tuned in. Don felt as if the room spun up and out. Floating down the street. He wished it would touch down somewhere away from the city. Somewhere Hawk could just let him outside anytime he wanted.

"Don, come here boy," Hawk called. Don hopped into Hawk's lap. He didn't know much about the clean spoon, the clean needle, or what it contained. He just looked in the pale, happy man's face and licked his hand.

If he could speak, Don wouldn't know what to say. Hawk always told him that words were a limiter. Words were the ultimate mediocrity of thoughts. Words served to quantify, qualify and limit what he knew. Don knew this too and licked him back in agreement.

Don wondered why Hawk insisted on playing the same record day after day. He couldn't place the music. But he knew that it was played over and over again at 33 1/3.

"Good boy, good." Hawk said. Don grew restless, fidgeting on his seat. Don's joy in Hawk's lap evaporated soon after it appeared.

Hawk continued to write in the notebook. Jabs of blue ink hit the page. Don never saw the words, but that was a gift. He wouldn't know what they meant and probably would not care for Hawk as much if he knew.

Don was a forgiving dog, with a short attention span and a long memory. For as long as Don could remember, the late afternoons were spent in this room with Hawk, the record, the needle, the spoon, and the black notebook that his owner locked away when he was done.

Hawk felt like a composer. He pulled the strings. He lifted the whole roof off the room. He filled the notebook with bright ink and warm words. He had pierced his eyes and heated his skin. Hawk's writing bubbled just underneath the point where it hurt. He guarded the border between real pain and pain that felt like heaven.

Taking a break from writing, Hawk conversed with himself in unwritten conversation. Don punctuated the silence with a sigh and shifted on the floor below.

The day had been dark and cool. The clouds hung low and mean across the autumn sky. Hawk's favorite time of year. When the outside world died from summer excess and dug in for long, cold sleep.

"Well, of course," Hawk said to himself. He smiled. There was no mirror in the room so only Don saw him smile. The smile curved inward and upward. It split open for a second to show the real stuff inside. The good shit.

Hawk needed this. He always did.

Weird conversations wigged him out. Even the routine ones. Still weird, all the time. The back and forth with a random dude when Hawk took a piss. With the flight attendant on the plane about cream in his coffee. With the ticket taker at the movies and his theater number and whether it was to the left or right. With the cab driver about his destination. With a tourist asking for directions to some place he only went when his relatives were in town. With some guy with a stylish haircut about a new pair of jeans.

He remembered one from earlier this afternoon on the way home.

"What a great choice. This sure does make me hungry," the grocery store clerk said as she placed his groceries into a paper bag. Hawk's was a Spartan sack with white rice, broccoli, two flank steaks, and green onions.

"Making dinner?"

Hawk nodded.

"For who?"

Hawk shrugged. He took the food and kept walking. He walked past the guy with the clipboard who asked him for a conversation about the environment. He was late to get back home and back to his room with his record player and Don.

"I saw you. Why did you say that?" Hawk said out loud to his stack of records. Don looked on. That's what he always wanted to say to Hawk. But Don was a dog and could not speak his language.

Hawk wrote in his notebook. He did this every afternoon for the same amount of time. He put his words in there, just for him. The record player stopped, just a faint click and pop of the needle at the end. He wondered how long it would do that. Infinitely. Or at least until the needle wore out. The music was his motor, so Hawk had to make sure that didn't happen.

He heard a knock at the door. It was patient, but repeated.

Knock. Knock. Knock. The sound was consistent and just loud enough to get his attention.

"One second," he replied.

Hawk drew a deep breath. He put the pen back in the coffee cup on the upper left side of his wooden desk. He opened the second drawer from the bottom on the right side of the desk. It slid open and he placed the notebook underneath a stack of old newspaper clippings. He closed the drawer and took the key that was sitting on top of the desk. He locked the drawer and put the key in his pocket.

Hawk stood up. He walked over to the record player and flipped the switch to OFF. He opened the plastic cover and picked up the black vinyl. He returned it to its sleeve and placed the album back on the shelf.

Hawk ran his hands through his hair. It was a little greasy, maybe he should wash it in the morning. He straightened his button-down shirt and adjusted his black pants, wiping off a few crumbs and strands of Don's coat. Hawk opened the door.

"Hiya, darling," she said. "How was tonight's album?"

"Good, babe. Really took me back. Just what I needed. There's nothing like a little aural therapy."

Hawk smiled and kissed her gently on the cheek. Don got up from the floor and walked down the hallway.

"Did you get the groceries for dinner?" she asked.

"Yeah, I can get it started. Hungry?" he said.

"Yeah, I could eat something," she responded.

"Cool," he said and walked out into the hallway.

Hawk closed the door behind him, walked into the kitchen and started preparing dinner.

"Baäl"
Exuma (1970)

Baäl was worshipped by the Canaanites. It's obvious that the Calypso rhythms do a solid job illuminating the meaning. Haunting does not justly describe this song. Shivers are a common reaction and the aching vocals illuminate visions of burnt wings, blown-out candles, and wind rushing in through a broken window.

Hearts can ache, hearts can be empty and it takes a bit of Bahamian magic to meld them together into a heady stew of rhythmic trance.

Dots

It was a very Virgo thing to think. Of course it was. She looked down through the clouds, through the electrical wires, through the wooden roofs and finally through the concrete walls. A clear view was sometimes the toughest one to find.

Her friends just saw dots. Sad dots, happy dots, rich dots, poor dots, dark dots, light dots and all dots in between. There were dots that lived in large dot houses without another dot in sight. Other dots were crammed together in a small space. One dot was way over there, among the dirt and trees, all by his dot-self. Some dots that were no longer living dots were buried deep below. Some dots lived in small dot settlements. Other dots lived in large dot places with metal buildings she could almost touch.

Most dots looked at the sky when they slept. Other dots looked down or to the side. Some dots told other dots to kill other dots. Other dots told other dots not to do this. Some dots took color and put it on a canvas to show other dots something that they thought was a unique dot thought. Some dots held other dots and wanted to do so forever. Some dots lived in places where other dots thought it was too remote for any dot to survive.

It was tough to remember them all, but Virgo always remembered: there are a lot of dots down there.

Was Virgo a little uptight? Most of her friends thought in strange ways about the dots. Some thought they were dirty. Others thought they were dangerous.

The simplest way to see the dots was just as dots. Some called them circles. Others called them spots. Virgo thought they were like rain drops. She called them drops, as each one was individual.

Sagittarius and Scorpio were the worst. But who could blame them? They always felt lonely and hung out to dry over the blue water. The few specks of land they saw were filled with emptiness or filled to the brim with dots that pushed up on one another. So many dots, that they would form their own shapes.

One night, Sagittarius screamed to Virgo, "Look, right there! Don't those dots look just like a horse?"

She sighed. "Of course they do, Sagittarius. Of course they do."

He went on a tangent about how the dots would be much better if they learned just a little from all the animals around them. Sagittarius loved the animals. They seemed so much more civilized and they never stared at the sky. It always felt like the dots were planning something. Virgo just assumed he was paranoid.

He could see her looking at his hooved half, but didn't care. That's not why he thought the dots looked like animals. He was sure he wasn't projecting. Those dots really did look like something.

At night, Scorpio and Sagittarius would lay on their backs, envisioning what shapes and creatures the dots could form. The birds always got in the way, but sometimes it was a horse. Other nights maybe a cow. Virgo would roll her eyes whenever they told her those stories about dots being formations with "special qualities." Each dot was special to her in its own way.

Virgo always thought that the darkness had its benefits, with its lack of rules and forever expansiveness. However, it was hard to be heard in the darkness, with no air.

One night. She looked down. Past the breaking waves, she stared both east and west and right into an open window inside one of those buildings where the dots live in rooms separated by walls on all sides. The setting sun had warmed up the dot's city and most of them were out on top of the buildings tonight or on the streets. Now that it was nighttime, the dark cast shadows on dots that pointed their fingers at tiny boxes. Sometimes they aimed these tiny boxes at other dots and the boxes captured a picture of these dots for future reference. Other dots started at these boxes as they walked down the street. Virgo thought this was dangerous, as some dots would run right into another dot or right into a tree, or their dot feet would trip on a piece of the dot trash that piled up in these large dot cities. The dots left a lot of trash up here in the sky too. Sagittarius hated trash.

Virgo saw into the room. She breathed deeply and took a few moments to understand the situation. Virgo's moments were longer and wider than thoughts. It may have taken more time, but could she feel deeper than dots? Or was it just different?

Virgo couldn't quite tell why, but for some reason, tonight felt different. She knew it must have been the room she was looking into.

The room with the open window had a dot inside, probably 18 or 19. Long hair, a deep medium brown, tied back in a tight bow. Virgo wondered if the dot was staring back at her. The dot's left eye squinted right at her.

Focusing her light downward, Virgo heard the dot's dot friends talking to her. Virgo listened as they talked about dot things. Mostly about their dot classes and their dot dreams. The dot that Virgo was fascinated with was talking about the stars and pointed right at Virgo and then at a few of her friends. The other dots seemed to focus their energies and only a couple of her dot friends yawned with boredom.

This dot had a fascination with the stars. A name for each group. Just like cells in the body, these stars fed the conversation she had with her dot friends.

Each night for the next week, Virgo followed her and her interest grew. It was too tough to see during the day, too bright. But each night, her eyes would follow the dot and her ears followed the dot's talk about stars and celestial matters. What she couldn't see, she pieced together from the dot's friends and their conversations. If she was very lucky, Virgo could squint and see the paper the dot was writing on. The dot would read cards with her friends and hear them talking. Virgo thought it was strange that the dots would always connect the stars with the day the dots were born from another dot. It confused her, but fascinated her at the same time. Scorpio never thought about one dot more than another. Sagittarius never thought about the dots as more than just dots. These dots were deep, this dot in particular.

Dots were funny too, Virgo thought. For every deep-thinking dot, there were a handful of shallow dots. Everyone was different, sort of like how she was different than Scorpio.

This dot was different, Virgo sensed it. That's why she followed her every night when she could.

Most dots never spent much time looking up. Sure, the dots looked around. They looked right. They looked left. They looked down, but rarely up. Up to the top of the dot buildings or that tower built by some dot with a lot of dot money, but not up up.

Another clear evening meant that Virgo could scan the scene. She loved to check on her favorite dot and see what she was up to. Virgo was bored up there, with only a couple of angry stars to keep her company.

Tonight, the dot was staring at her, right? This dot made Virgo feel insecure about the whole thing, because the dot could see right through her, past the darkness. This dot seemed free from the other dots.

The dot was by herself tonight on the top of her dot building. Virgo thought that her friends must have been up to other dot activities. This was a special night and Virgo could feel it.

This dot opened a dot box and pulled out an elongated metal device. Virgo had seen them in all shapes and sizes before, but this one seemed old, at least in dot years. The dot put this device on a tripod and angled it up at Virgo.

The dot looked in and Virgo could at once see her right eye. Virgo thought it was a beautiful eye. The dot smiled and Virgo tried winking back. Had the dot seen this?

The dot came back to the same spot on clear nights and Virgo looked forward to this. She never told Sagittarius, Scorpio, or any of her other comrades in space. They didn't need to know. Virgo and this dot looked in each other's eyes. They shared the same wide moment.

"She Lives (In a Time of Her Own)"
The 13th Floor Elevators (1967)

A thumper with thin drums and celestial lyrics. Think about the concept of time. This song is another way of drawing a circle around it. The guitar, drums and vocals come together in a knot that you see and immediately understand, but you never know quite how they did it.

The electric jug starts in the back of the mix, but whirls and swirls at just the right moments. The cymbals punctuate in a fuzzy clang. Less a song and more an electric wave that has been flying through inner space for eternity.

Ghost Connection

Day 1

Deep stood staring at the matted red carpet on the wall. The ground looked dirty and the short carpet on the floor had lost its color years ago.

Deep could feel it. The music seeping out of his fingers. The song. THE song. All he had to do was write it.

His black, straw-thin hair swayed. Did this windowless room have a draft? Did someone slam a door somewhere in this converted warehouse? Either way, the air whispered through his hair, enhancing Deep's melodic trance.

He felt it coming on and over him, like bleach spiking his cerebellum.

Deep sat on the floor, dirt and dust tickling his ankles. He stared at his amp, a refurbished Orange tube. The perfect tone with a hint of English fuzz. Deep stared off again. This time, he closed his eyes. The notes, the music, the verse and the chords painted the inside of his eyelids. His mind grasped for a pen, but Deep knew he was hugging a ghost. The embrace appeared, then it disappeared. Then it reappeared, but further away.

Deep picked up his guitar, a sunburst Gibson SG. He fingerpicked to get the ghost back. That's where he started. Strumming a few notes, then a few more. His phone rang in his pocket. He put down the guitar. Its neck nestled in the red shag carpet on the wall. The guitar's silence slammed against the wall.

Deep looked at his phone; Cherry was calling. A total babe. Deep loved the way she looked. They had met a few months back at an after-party. They had shared thoughts since that meeting that connected them. They felt together, whether they were a few hours or a few miles apart. Deep craved the killer connection with Cherry and their melting minds.

"Hiya, darling," he drawled. Cherry thought his drawl was hot, even if he was from Michigan.

"Hey," she shot back. Her voice sounded tense. Cherry's red lip and frizzed, pink hair hid a voice that screamed suburbia.

"What's wrong?" Deep's mind churned. Was it the night before? His head ached from the cheap beer and whiskey shots. But the boys wanted to go out and she said she didn't mind. But did she? Deep needed to keep the boys nice and loose, she knew that. They worked better that way.

"I don't know." Cherry replied, her voice tensing more with each syllable.

"Well, do you want me to come over?" Deep searched.

"Maybe?"

Deep questioned what Cherry was getting at.

"Ok. I'll call you in a little while."

"Just text me."

"Are you sure?"

"Yeah."

"Ok."

"Bye."

Deep picked up the guitar off the floor. His mind drifted. He thought about this morning when he woke up and the early morning before he went to sleep.

Focus, Deep thought. He strummed notes and looked at the drum set and the empty throne. He had played the translucent blue drums last night, but the whole thing made the space empty. He missed Rusty's rhythms. No one relied on Rusty, but Deep relied on his drums.

Deep laid the guitar down and lit a cigarette. What was a song? Deep dreamt of chords. Melodies. Bridges. A truss double deck or a regular drawbridge?

He exhaled and spit a speck of tobacco on the floor from the corner of his mouth. Smoke trailed out his nostrils as he sat there thinking about the song. Cherry hated it when Deep smoked. She thought it was relic.

He picked the guitar off the floor for the final time just as his phone rang in his left pocket. Deep threw the phone on the ground, stood up and hit the high hat with his free hand, producing a muted but jarring noise in the empty room.

"Hiya, darling," Deep said, picking up the phone. His breath was a little short.

"Come and see me," Cherry said. Her voiced produced a steamed-powered strength that Deep liked.

"Alright."

He put the guitar down and off he went. He had not done much tonight, but he promised to himself that he would return in better form tomorrow. He closed his eyes and the ghost vanished. The song drifted down the road. The melody turned her back.

Day 2

Deep stayed in his apartment for most of the day before heading out to the practice space. He feared the city's concrete during the day. A storm rolled in that afternoon followed by a turbulent night. Time crept past midnight as he unlocked the deadbolt on the practice space. He slept a little too much. His mind sloshed with memories of recent conversations.

He rested his hand on the red shag carpet covering the walls, his hand sunk in past his first knuckles. Soft, synthetic strands pulsed on his skin. His own strands of long black hair shook. Deep felt something. The connection. The conversation behind the wall. The misplaced wires behind the wall. He didn't know the source of energy, but didn't need to.

He closed his eyes and picked up his guitar. The colors of melody and harmony illuminated the darkened practice space. With no drummer or bassist, Deep felt more like a mystic or a monk. He played away and after a few minutes, poured himself whiskey from a flask in his boot.

The cords wove together and interlocked patterns of unexplored shapes and colors. He touched the patterns with his eyes and tasted the colors with his mind. He felt his leg vibrate. It was Cherry.

"Whatcha doing?" Cherry asked. Noise spilled through her phone. A phone handled only so much noise. Deep could handle less. Glasses, laughter, music and random chatter. Cherry drank tonight as she did last night. Loud and in quantity.

"Working," Deep said. He wanted to get this over with as soon as he could.

"Oh, come on, don't be so fucking boring," Cherry hurled back at him.

"Boring?" Deep pretended.

"What?"

"Huh?"

They went on like that for a little while, testing out each other's hearing through their phones.

"Come down, please."

"Alright, just give me a few."

He closed his eyes. The ghost had fled. The melody had vanished, took off further down the road. Somewhere, Deep knew he could find it.

Day 3

Deep walked in to the practice space with his mind muddled. Someone had left the door unlocked. He shared it with some reggae fusion band. Not the best band, but they kept it clean and paid on time. The ultimate stoner surprise.

Deep drank long and deep. He picked up the guitar and played. He tested three pieces of his song. He strummed and hummed along. Verse-Chorus-Verse-Bridge and then Deep stopped. He had not finished the song so Deep went deeper.

He reconstructed the ghost. His bands could never illuminate a crowd. At best, they could flicker.

His fingers pulled his hair behind his ears. He strummed the guitar and closed his eyes. A dozen hands of various shapes grabbed his mind. Deep cleared the fog bank and the ghost stood there, waiting for him.

Deep had captured the ghost or she had captured him. Either way, for the next three minutes, he had it. The song flowed out in fuzz. Deep had plugged into the well. The song ran out down the hall. Deep envisioned the voltage running through to another room, through the ground. Through the sea, the mantle, the center of the Earth and back to the surface, where some upside-down person could feel the fuzz in reverse.

Time stretched and Deep's hands held the ghost again and again. It was effortless. The ghost was running through outer space, pulling Deep with her.

The dark room glowed from the humming Orange amp. The buzz in his pocket. It was Cherry. He didn't answer it. He knew what she wanted.

Deep put down his guitar. He closed his eyes and saw nothing but the three vertical colors painted on his mind. He closed the door and locked the deadbolt. Ghosts never last long, but this ghost lasted long enough to remember.

"Whiskey Woman"
Flamin Groovies (1971)

A pure-grained raga from start to finish. So strong and stoned—we can only dream what it would've been like if this song had rocketed to the top of the charts. If we could spin the planet backwards, this song would add another ring around Saturn and balance the lost lands of wrong times and what ifs.

Once the reverse orbit is completed, we are left with this still-smoking, fried San Francisco rock 'n roll. Rough and raw, the driving drums expanding space into five directions and breathing life between the beats and searing dual guitars. Drink it slow. Drink it long. But don't forget to drink it all up.

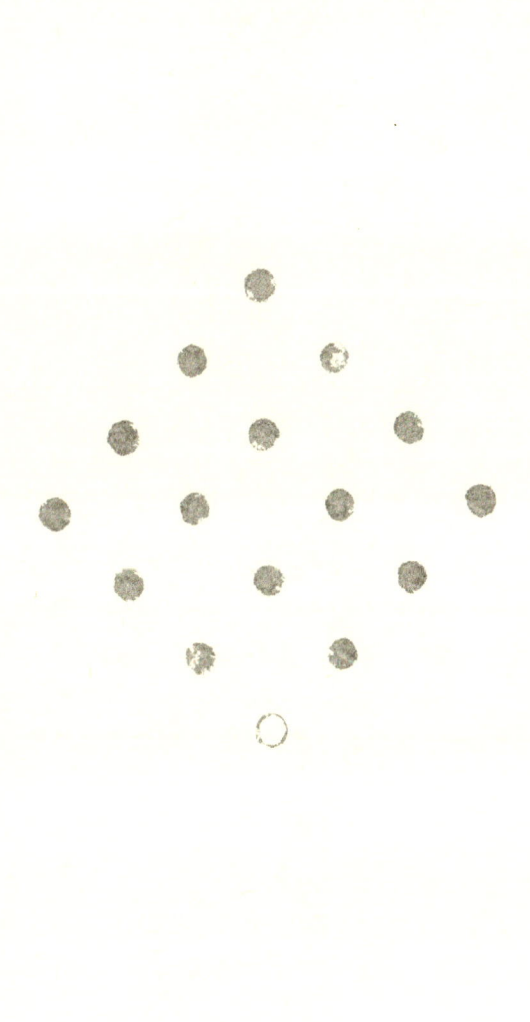

Ions on Fire

Sage stretched out his hand. His hair ruffled a bit and stuck up straight. It was like thin, black sticks pushing out of their skins.

The sun had set a few hours ago. The clouds hung on the horizon, but he could already embrace them. A dark green haze plastered the bottom of the now-dark sky. Sage pushed down the road, knowing that the green would give way to darkness darker than the night itself.

The highway split into two lanes. One moving forward. One moving backwards. Each intersecting street did the same thing, splitting off in two different directions. It stretched out forever into nothingness with two choices.

Sage's car shimmied as his right foot pressed down on the gas pedal. It was not the most prime machine on the planet, but it looked good. A faded black 1979 Dodge Magnum with more miles than stories, but also more problems than its exterior let on. Sage knew how to drive the beast, but he didn't like to think about how it was going to go.

The metal, bolts and gasoline of the 1979 Dodge Magnum moved in a straight line with Sage's records, his clothes, and a few other things in the trunk. This machine got the job done.

"Ahhh," Sage screamed and shook his head.

Sage lacked machismo most of the time, but not when he was behind the wheel on the open road. He loved to scream, so he let out another one. Loudly. In the car all by himself.

He screamed "Yeeeeaaahhhh." The tone pierced his ears and was a little higher pitched than he had hoped for.

The car flew down the road, locked in rhythm with Sage's screams. Other than his vocal chords letting out a strained "Yeeeaahhh," it was silent in the car. Sage's packed clothes, records, weed and the other assorted things he'd dragged down from his room didn't say a word.

He felt like big, bright eyes were probing the car every so often. Sometimes it was just one and other times it was a few right in a row. Bright, orange eyes that would shine in his car. He told himself it was just the street lights, which were becoming fewer and fewer the further he got out.

Sage's car stereo was busted, but the car made its own music. It grunted, groaned and moaned on the highway at just above the speed limit. Sage looked around at the trees and scrub mountains. He had a friend somewhere in the mountains. Or down here. Or back at home. Somewhere was Sage's friend. He just couldn't remember at that moment. The car sped by and the eyes in the darkness kept their pupils on Sage.

"Ahhhhhhhhh," Sage's voice lifted. Onward.

It had been a long day. Sage remembered this road, but was a little hazy on the destination. This adventure reminded him of a book he read in class. He could not recall the name, but it was one of those great novels with many editions and the footnotes about history and references in the back.

Sage took the one-hitter out of the ashtray and, with one hand, packed it full of pot. It was from his friend, but it was not the best stuff he'd ever had. Balancing the small, metal pipe on his lap, he grabbed the lighter and picked up the one hitter, placing it in his mouth. He lit it and saw his reflection, but turned his eyes back to the road. He took one more hit and put it back in the ashtray. This time, he held the smoke in just a bit longer than the first and exhaled. The car flew down the road.

Feeling calmer, Sage knew that he was almost where he wanted to be. Somewhere in those hills around him where it wasn't so dark and there were no bright, orange eyes staring at you from above. Somewhere where he wanted to be and not back where his parents lived.

Sage had always wanted a girlfriend named Lucille. A dog named Dale. A cabin with one room, framing one naked light bulb and one modest bed. Shangri-La in the hills. Damp and true without the nothingness. Nobody got that. Not his parents. Not Mary, his girlfriend. Not Charlie, the family dog. Charlie fucking hated Sage. Can't really blame him though. Charlie was the most instinctual in the family.

Sage didn't always make a whole lot of sense. He remembered the guitar he loved to play. But that romance was brief. After seeing The Shivers in some basement with a dozen other dudes, he took the twelve-string and smashed it against his wall. His parents looked the other way. Mary walked away. Charlie barked. Charlie fucking hated Sage. He barked again, for added effect. Sage always felt uncomfortable around Charlie. His eyes were pinned on Sage like he knew what he was thinking.

Sage didn't feel that many people understood him. Sure, he had his friends, getting high, laughing and fooling around, but did they really know him? Sometimes he would see them talking and all the words sounded like some other language. Just tones and grunts that meant nothing. He was just complicating his mind and after this one-hitter, it felt more and more like mush. It was all questions, big and small, at the moment.

"Ahhhhhh," Sage pushed on.

The darkness complemented the highway, wrapping around it in slimming fashion. The car's headlights formed a halo around it. The street lights were long gone on this stretch of highway. The land was darkness, in the middle of a more complete, soulless black. A storm black. The black became light when thunder shook parts of the darkness that were further away. But Sage knew that the storm black was coming for him.

He didn't mind the storm until the rain came. Lightening and thunder made music for Sage and added eerie effects to his nighttime ride. Some foreign spice tossed into his homemade soup. Sage didn't cook, but he thought about adding something else to his mind. He did that a lot.

He packed the one hitter again, but was more careful this time. The rain had started to come down and he didn't want to become a poster child for getting high and driving. Sage lit the one hitter again and took it all in at once. He held it in and blew a decent cloud of smoke. It danced with the lightening on the horizon and slipped out the window. The smoke was running for the hills too. Sage thought about that for a few minutes, but realized he needed to take a piss.

Sage pulled over a few minutes later at the first stop. He turned his right blinker on as he pulled into the gas station. He knew the car had more than enough in the tank, but he needed to piss and the rain was now coming down in sheets.

As Sage got out, he thought that he might be here for a little bit. Sage drove as well as he rebelled, so his skills would be suspect in this storm. The 1979 Dodge Magnum was not one for the elements either. It fogged up in heavy rain and the engine would squeal and the tires would wobble on slippery footing.

Sage put his one hitter and the weed back in the ashtray and got out of the car. He stepped in the mud and locked the door.

"Hey," he said to the man behind the gas station counter. The dude nodded back. Sage stopped for a second, but realized the dude behind the counter didn't really respond to him. His eyes were glued to his cell phone and the security camera that kept watch over this gas station.

Sage bought a black coffee, a 24-ounce can of beer, a bag of salted peanuts, some orange-flavored sugar slices and two tins of potato chips.

"$12.88," said the man behind the counter. Sage handed him a $20 bill. He loved using cash, it made him feel real. Or at least real-ish. The dude gave Sage $7.12 in change. The dude then reached behind the counter and put his beer, peanuts, orange candy and potato chips into a plastic bag. He handed it to Sage who grabbed the bag and the black coffee off the counter.

Sage backed out and pulled around. He paused for a few seconds and put on his left blinker, pulling out onto the highway. The yellow line went both ways and Sage thought about how far he could go in either direction.

Today blurred back and forth in his mind. Sage crashed down the stairs with his green duffle bag. He had thrown some clothes in along with a couple of his dad's records. Sage remembered that memories were strong at the moment, but they weakened over time.

"AHHHHHHHIIIII," Sage screamed.

The road straightened out on this stretch of the journey and Sage still didn't feel those eyes staring at him. Every so often, a slight bend or a hill would provide entertainment as the other cars shot their headlights into the air. The light bent and went straight into Sage's eyes.

An hour or so later, the cars started to enter the roadway. At first from side roads and then from everywhere. The road turned into two lanes, then three, and then the streetlights illuminated the scene. The buzz of the city surrounded Sage, who cruised at a slower clip than the other cars.

Sage and the 1979 black Dodge Magnum pulled back into the driveway. His dad would call it a sideways park job. Charlie barked at Sage. Charlie fucking hated him.

Sage slung his records over his shoulder and took the green duffel bag with his clothes up the stairs. His dad stopped him on the stairs and inspected the records in the bag hanging on his son's shoulder.

"Hey, that's my record," his dad reminded.

"Yeah," Sage said.

"Well, just so you know," his dad responded.

Sage shrugged. What did his dad know about music anyway, he thought as he slammed the door to his room.

"Medication"
The Chocolate Watch Band (1968)

A perfect groove down a dark highway. A tale of drug love sung by a cretin combo from the Bay Area suburbs. Who knows how people thought of them, but San Jose's favorite Stones brought it heavy and heady in healthy doses. Of all their tunes, this one sticks in my mind like few others have. While the band was known for their massive covers of British bands, this one could stand on its own West Coast pedigree as the band grew out and about among the trees.

Maybe you've been there, driving in circles and staring at the ever-expanding darkness. On a dark road and sometimes you need a little something to clear the mind and light the pavement moving forward.

A Turn Above

This water was magical at any time of day.

Whether it was morning, and the sun rose over the green hillside and reflected towards the clouds, waking the sea's slumber. Whether it was midday, as the heat started to boil the sun. Whether it was late afternoon, as the beach quieted and people hung on to that last swim, that last beer, or that last strong ray of sunshine. Whether it was evening, as the moon replaced the sunlight that baked the sea blue every day.

Today was no different.

These boats were magical too.

Whether it was the public ferries shuffling the people about in a hypnotic rhythm punctuated with belches of exhaust. Whether it was a yacht owned by a rich Arabian prince, standing on his gilded floating palace. Whether it was the ghosts of the sailboats that used to sail on these waters, seeking romance, wealth and adventure. Whether it was the boats rented by drunk Americans or Australians, who took advantage of the relaxed boating and liability laws in Italy. These boats carried wine, dreams and a pair or two of black designer sunglasses.

Today, Dusty and Darling, two American tourists from the West Coast, chartered one of these boats. They were visiting this cove, stuck between trees, rocks and ocean, cut off from cars and trucks. As remote as you can get along the coast of Italy in July. This place felt as romantic as one needed it to be. The waves balanced everything, pulsing towards the shore—clear, blue and violent.

The engine purred and the sound rose and fell against the waves. As they came closer to the shore, the captain cut the engine, letting the water take them in. The boat bobbed, but neither of them seemed to mind. Darling talked to Dusty the way that husbands on vacations do. Loving with an added air of excitement. Their conversations were brash, fierce and fun on this trip.

Maybe it was the local fish they ordered last night at the restaurant, baked in salt and caught a few miles from where they were. Maybe it was the memory of their cab driver, a beautiful, brawny Italian who wore faded jeans and obnoxious sneakers. He wore them well, due to his magnificent hair and charming accent. Maybe it was the bar chiseled into rock where they had a final drink. Maybe it was the kiss they shared with Dusty pressed against the stairwell of the three-story hotel they were staying in on the hills overlooking the water. Maybe it was the joint they shared before midnight still on the tips of their tongues. Maybe it was the booze from Dusty and Darling's morning cocktails as they sat near a pool and ate pastries, hard cheese and yogurt.

The water mixed in their eyes. Darling and Dusty's eyes reflected the water and turned from green to deep blue.

The waves rose as the sun flashed down. Darling looked at the tanned captain and swore he saw his skeleton. The captain smiled back.

"Can he see mine?" Darling wondered.

Dusty wore a short dress with vertical blue stripes against a white background. Her boating outfit complimented the shoeless Darling and his pair of faded blue jeans and a short-sleeve, button-down shirt that hung easily over his slight frame. He ached like a middle-aged man, but Darling didn't mind. He liked growing old.

He spotted two young men in white suits rowing towards their boat.

"You go," said the tanned Italian captain with the inside-out skeleton. Darling smiled back and put a few euros in his palm after shaking his hand.

The captain had a certain air. He knew commanding respect was a form of currency, but pocketed Darling's euros anyways.

The young men's boats glided along the water and their beauty was not hard for Dusty to notice.

Could they see her staring? Do they get off on that? Darling thought to himself.

The last few meters felt like a gift. Their upper arms glistened as they reached out and helped Darling and Dusty aboard their dingy. Darling's only nautical flair was one of those silly sailor caps with an anchor on it. It fell off his head and into the water, but floated right back to the surface. Once Darling was seated, one of the boys scooped it out, shook it a few times and handed it back to him.

Darling and Dusty rode to shore like King and Queen. The Italians on the shore didn't see it that way, but they were happy to play along. Smiling and waving, the older men tanned their hairy chests.

Darling and Dusty strode on the beach. The two young men in white suits tipped their hats and were off again to pick up the next pair of regal tourists bobbing up and down in the placid water.

The cove only had one beach, accessible by foot or by boat. Darling and Dusty had been there on their honeymoon many moons ago and this corner of land felt lost in time. The little restaurant, the old church, the old men and the sand. It felt the same as when they'd left years ago.

Dusty saw the restaurant and went inside. The brightness outside was no friend to the dark, cool climate of this rock-sided bar. The people inside were less friendly to

Darling than he remembered. They smiled as they pulled the beer to their lips, but shrugged when he spit out his English words at them. It took him three or four minutes until the only waitress who spoke English stuck her head outside and waved him on to sit at a table shaded by a ragged tree.

Rust. The color of afternoon. The color of faded greatness. The color of what is and what could have been. The color of what had happened. The color of time.

Darling thought about this as the sun played tricks on the sand, turning it from a whitish yellow to rust and turning the greens darker, the water bluer and taking everything from where it was, to a turn above.

Darling and Dusty sat comfortably at their table. The shade of the tree kept the sun from making them look older. She smiled at him and wished he could be the man who brought them there years ago, when they were younger and had fewer wrinkles at the corners of their eyes. The charming, younger man who had less money but more morning. Darling looked at Dusty and wished he could be that younger man whose passion was adventure and whose love was everything at that very moment. He should have written a book about that man.

Dusty and Darling could hear songs swirling in their ears as they waited for their food, but there was no music at the restaurant and the only music on the beach was the noise leaking out from an older man's headphones. Dusty and Darling heard the songs that they used to love.

They talked. Not like they talked at home, but like they thought they talked at home. The conversation burrowed to the bottom of the sea, but stayed bright like a finger barely reaching to the sun.

Cycles and cycles of conversations, salads and drinks and antipasti and wine, followed by more words and dreams and glances. A man with a thick, drunken English accent interrupted them.

He rambled on about this special restaurant, nestled on the north Italian coast. A coast where sailors once sailed and people had loved and lived for years buried on years. He told Dusty and Darling about wisdom, about his family who seemed to consist of sullen teenagers fathered by another man and a bored Russian wife. His family spoke no English and was less interested in talking to him. Because of this, he spoke too much to Dusty and Darling. Despite his desperation, Darling and Dusty enjoyed his company. Especially because he ordered a bottle of wine to their table.

The Englishman, who never told them his name, shook their hands and half-hugged Darling's wife. He spoke at length to them about his mother, like they were brothers, but the couple could not envision what she looked like. Dusty gathered from the surroundings, the age of the man and his drunken persona, that he must have come from some sort of wealth, but how much was left was really a private matter for this Englishman, his Russian wife and the two kids from another man. The kids listened to their devices with white headphones in their ears, escaping a place they could care less for.

After the Englishman left with his Russian wife, Dusty and Darling settled in with a little more wine. They talked about past happenings, but really it was less the words and more the feeling between them. A silence hung over their table and held both of them. Dusty and Darling were still in love after all these years and the silence between them was comforting.

A light dessert of sweets and bitter coffee followed their wine and everything felt like a cloud.

They walked down the beach and to the dock. Darling held Dusty's hand like a lover does and kissed it. Dusty shimmered in the light as they waited for the young men in the white suits to row their way.

"Acqua azzurra, acqua chiara"
Lucio Battisti (1970)

This song about the sea dances like waves. Translated to "Blue Water, Clear Water," the words envision Italian seas that lazily lap against the shore with those tanning, eating and relaxing.

This song is the essence of the power of music. Words mixing with the lush instrumentation to create a sound that speaks for itself and speaks to you, whether you're an Italian or from lands across the sea.

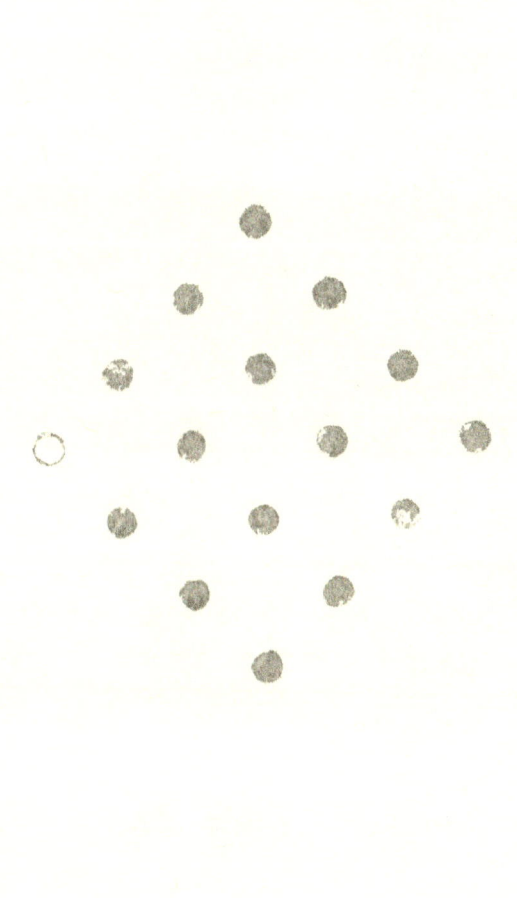

Best to Move

It is a cold, crisp start to a new day. The air bites through my clothes. The street lamps illuminate the surroundings, bathing everything in orange. The dirty streetlights mix with headlights, apartment lights and office lights. It adds a little grit to a city feeling more and more like an amusement park.

No one is finding the moon tonight, it's nowhere to be found. The stars hide on a clear night too. Sometimes no one feels like going out. The moon and stars want to stay in tonight and eat cosmic popcorn in tin foil.

It's a little after 3:00am and I'm on my nightly walk through the city. After the bars close, after the kids go back home or to an after-party or to fill their faces, this is my time. I finish my joint. It helps even out my mood and I plant myself between the dirt and the firmament of the skyscrapers.

The manhole covers cough smoke that swirls upward, helped by the cabs and cars passing by. It all swirls around into a cloud that smells like sex, industry, oil and nothingness. A sweet, but acquired taste.

I have been writing all night and drinking cheap Italian wine. A little tip for aspiring alcoholics: pick out the bottle at the corner store by balancing out the old-world charm of the label with the alcoholic content. It takes a sort of Zen, but this balance will get the job done.

I zip up my leather jacket. I've pinned a couple of band buttons to it. My outfit is completed with a pair of narrow, leather walking boots, black action slacks, and a t-shirt underneath. Perfect for this late spring evening.

Some people walk to clear their head. The air provides perspective on their lives. Some people walk for exercise. Pumping blood, burning off calories and all that. Some people walk because they don't or won't own a car. These people don't want to pay for a cab or ride on the subway. Some people can't walk at all, but wheel down the streets instead. Some people walk with their dogs, then take a break and wait for the dog to take a shit. Some people walk because they are trying to walk things off. Walking off a drunk, a breakup, or just too many thoughts in their head.

Me? I just like to walk. It's a good thing. It's the silence that grabs me.

I see a girl on the other side of the street. It has been a few months since my girlfriend moved out, so while I won't say I'm "looking," it never hurts to turn my head at the right one. She looks cute in a plain, intriguing way. All black clothing and black hair too. She seems to be looking at the wall. Maybe it's a flyer. Maybe she likes to collect records or maybe she likes to listen to the radio. I slow down and there she is, staring at the wall. I make out only the left side of her face. The streetlights bathe her face in orange hues, but I continue walking.

Some people walk with others in large groups or small groups. Some people walk in pairs, holding hands and looking into each other's eyes. Some people walk in groups of three or even four. Some people split their larger group into two groups of two or, if there is an odd person out, three people and one person.

I always like being that one person.

Some people walk alone. Some people like to do something when walking. Some people talk on the phone while walking. These people have conversations with their mother, brother, boyfriends, ex-boyfriends, but mostly just their friends. These people sometimes talk to themselves and just pretend that there is another person on the line. Some people walk while listening to music. Some people walk and read on their phones. I keep a close eye out for these people to avoid any sidewalk accidents.

I look back and see the same girl, still on the other side of the street. Parallel paths, it seems. She walks forward now, so the orange light shines on her right side. I think it is just as good as the left. She stuns me. She's dressed in all black, but I can tell from her face that she's thinking about something deep. Maybe it's the flyer she looked at earlier. Maybe she walks to think about things like this. Her black hair blends perfectly with the evening and her bangs make her haunting in a hypnotizing way.

I can't help wondering if this is just the way I walk. The point of this whole routine.

It's much better at night. A lot less people walking, of all types. At this time of night, the streets are only for the people who like to walk or don't have another option.

The cars flash by, with dark interiors. Outside are two beams. Inside is a soft leather backseat.

I walk down the street and see more people than most nights. Mostly in groups of twos or threes, stumbling and talking. A few smoke cigarettes together, but mostly they are in their own stories, creating, reliving and creating again. Some people stumble towards exits and some people stumble inside.

I like to walk in a straight line, keep my head down and look up at just the right moment. Sort of like how I swim: Poorly, but good enough to never drown.

I try not to look into places where I'm not going and instead focus on where I am going. Sometimes it's easier to think that than to do it. I walk by two different apartments, one with a light on and a TV on in the room. I light a cigarette and pause. Just one look. I might see something for my book. That's what I always tell myself.

No one seems to be in the room and I'm the closest one to the television, which is playing sports highlights. A basketball game. I draw a drag and start walking again.

Best to move.

Streets act funny at night. Traffic lights, walk signals and traffic signs rest. They shift into strong suggestions rather than hard facts. A red light no longer means stop. The red hand asks you to look both ways. I always listen, especially for those drunks driving at this time of night.

I walk on.

The smell of Turkish food runs up my nose. I remember reading somewhere that smelling something is when a little piece of that something works its way into you. That's great when it's the smell of good food. Not so great when it's the smell of shit or death. But the bad smells make this city so great to walk in. They beat the city's heart and spin the buildings around.

Maybe this girl is going to have some food? Maybe? She doesn't even glance at the food stands. She walks on, still on the other side of the street. She keeps a steady pace with her black sneakers and white shoelaces. She still seems to be thinking deeply. I sort of lean into the street, thinking if I strain just a little, I could hear what she was thinking beneath her black bangs.

Sometimes on my walks, I'll walk by a beautiful girl or two. Their smell always catches me in just the right way and as soon as I catch it, she's gone. Smell hooks deeper than a glance of eyes. It is an elusive sense, always tricking the mind into where it wants you to go.

I remember this whenever I visit my parents or my friends who live outside the city. I'll take walks late at night. I enjoy walking outside the city, it's different. Fewer people diminishes to nobody. The darkness is everywhere and streetlights can be hard to find. Sidewalks can be harder to find, and walking on the street's shoulder makes a walker feel like his car must have broke down a few miles back down the road.

The bars always wiggle when they close. Some bars keep going. If I walk earlier, I see beer lights and pool tables. In the dead of night, the only places open are the ones that have light pouring underneath the door or light held behind thick, dark curtains. I couldn't care less about the worlds inside those mysteries.

While I walk in a straight line, I end up on a loop or an oval. I've never really drawn it out on a map, so I'm not sure what my walks look like. More and more, tonight's walk looks like two straight lines never to cross. I think about this more and more. What do I do?

This heavy thought weighs me down. I stop. What should I do? If I cross the street, would she run? If I don't do anything, does she just turn into vapor and melt away?

"Hey," she says.

"Hey," I muster back.

She has come across the street and now stands between the darkness and the orange. Beautiful and plain in all black, she intrigues me.

"Want to go for a walk?" she asks.

"Sure."

"We Will Fall"
The Stooges (1967)

A song that will let you inside it, slipping into the muck. A dark, deep escapade. Held in place with chants and sparse percussion, it takes a few listens, but dig in. Dig in deep.

Nocturnal introspection at the depths of the soul. A song for the ages and a break from their glorious broken bottles and beauty in chaos, the sounds are focused and flowing, and carry you down a spiral and into the black beyond.